C000150203

These pictures are for
Ann and the boys
These words are for Claude

Puffin Books, Penguin Books Ltd, Harmondsworth, Middlesex, England
Viking Penguin Inc., 40 West 23rd Street, New York, New York 10010, U.S.A.
Penguin Books Australia Ltd, Ringwood, Victoria, Australia
Penguin Books Canada Ltd, 2801 John Street, Markham, Ontario, Canada L3R 1B4
Penguin Books (N.Z.) Ltd, 182-190 Wairau Road, Auckland 10, New Zealand

First published by Hutchinson Junior Books Ltd 1979
First published 1987 in Pocket Puffins
by Puffin Books in association with Moonlight Publishing Ltd
Copyright © illustrations Reg Cartwright, 1979
Copyright © text Hutchinson Junior Books Ltd, 1979

All rights reserved

Made and printed in Italy by La Editoriale Libraria

MR POTTER'S
PIGEON

illustrations by Reg Cartwright
text by Patrick Kinmonth

Mr Potter lived quietly by himself at 35 Station Road, near the railway line. At the back of his house there was a garden where nettles, dock, cow parsley and tall foxgloves grew thickly in the shade. Mr Potter was not very interested in weeding. At the end of the garden was a shed, but there were no rakes, spades, wheelbarrows or oil cans in it because Mr Potter kept something much more important there: his racing pigeon.

One Friday evening Mr Potter walked slowly down the brick path to his shed. He often went there when the garden was falling still, and told the pigeon about the things that were on his mind.

Tonight he was thinking of the big race to be held on Sunday. When pigeons race they are put into their cages, carried far away and then set free. The pigeon which can find its way home most quickly is the winner.

Mr Potter was longing for his pigeon to win, but she was young and the others were fast, 'and every pigeon', he said, 'does not win the race'. Mr Potter was a man of few words. His friends sometimes asked him why he looked so sad, and he would say that is was only his moustache. He had an old photograph of his father who had a grey moustache and looked sad too, 'and he was smiling at the time', said Mr Potter.

That night the chimney cast its shadow like a dark blue ruler down the slates of the roof; the moon was full and bright. Mr Potter was sitting safe in his kitchen, but outside something was moving from shadow to shadow in the dark garden. Over by the shed the tall leaves of the iris bed rustled mysteriously, then they were parted by two cold, clear eyes that glittered like glass lemons in the moonlight. It was Lupin, the cat from next door. Without a sound he slid into the shed where Mr Potter's pigeon was asleep.

The tip of Lupin's long black tail twitched from side to side as he sat quite still beneath the sleeping pigeon's cage: then he leaped. His claws caught the metal latch, the door sprang open and Mr Potter's pigeon awoke with a start. She glanced at the shape of Lupin crouched below her, eyes blazing, and with sudden, clattering wings she flew over his head and out into the clear night sky, leaving Lupin amazed and striking at the empty air with flashing claws.

Mr Potter's pigeon rose high above the village and the moon seemed bright and close. Below her the railway lines shone like tight wires, and they led her to a curving river that reflected the dark trees along its banks. She flew down its silver course through strange fields and silent woods, and saw a line like the blade of a knife lying on the horizon; there was a sharp taste in the air, and she heard a low whispering sound—it was the sea.

A beam of light swept over the waves and vanished. Then it came again and was gone again, and again came and again was gone, a shaft of light shining out to sea. On a rock surrounded by foam and roaring waves stood a tall lighthouse. The tired pigeon dropped out of the sky like a soft stone on to a narrow window ledge, and fell asleep. All through the night the lighthouse flashed its warning out across the empty sea, while far away and warm in bed Mr Potter slept, untroubled.

Mr Potter's pigeon awoke before dawn. It was cold, and a bitter wind blew around the lighthouse. She looked out at the sea; the waves were empty except for a small black fishing boat on its way home. She looked towards the land and the hills rose comfortingly, with trees and church spires pointing to the village where she belonged. That was enough. As the sun rose, she left the lighthouse behind her and set off to find the way home to Mr Potter.

Mr Potter was having his breakfast when he suddenly dropped his spoon. The shed—he had forgotten to shut the door the night before! He ran down the red brick path and found the pigeon's cage open, empty except for one grey feather. 'Oh no', groaned Mr Potter. He could not believe it, and he stared at the cage, expecting the pigeon to appear at any moment. But she did not. Mr Potter fetched his binoculars and looked worriedly at the sky. A voice in his head said, 'She has gone for good', but he kept on looking.

Hours passed and the sun grew hot, so he took off his jacket and put on a sunhat made from a folded page of the newspaper. 'Oh dear,' said Mr Potter sadly to himself. 'You can't win a pigeon race without a pigeon, you know.'

Lupin walked across the garden and rubbed himself against Mr Potter's legs, purring loudly. Mr Potter bent down and stroked him. 'A cat will always be a cat,' he observed with a long sigh. Just as he was thinking that Lupin looked especially well-fed, Mr Potter heard a whirring of wings above him and he looked up eagerly. There was his pigeon sitting calmly on the roof of the shed, as if she had never been away. Mr Potter raised his hands, the pigeon flew down into them, and he pressed her soft grey back against his cheek. 'You've come back for the race, then?' he said with a chuckle, and the pigeon blinked her beady black eyes.

That night Mr Potter slept well. He dreamed that his pigeon asked him to fly with her, and they soared over a rainbow in the sky.

On the day of the race Mr Potter got up at five o'clock and put his pigeon into a wicker travelling basket. He looked up at the mantelpiece and imagined how a silver cup would look beside his father's photograph. 'Very nice indeed', said Mr Potter as he went down to the station. 'It would be nice to win'.

It was six o'clock when he arrived on the platform. The train was due to leave at ten past six to take the pigeons on their long journey to the starting place, but Mr Potter waited with his pigeon on his knees until the guard came and put her carefully inside and blew his whistle. Mr Potter felt that he was losing her again. 'She'll be all right', the guard said as the train left the station with a blast of steam.

When everything was ready the race began. Mr Potter's pigeon flew out of her basket, but to her surprise she found a thick grey fog was hiding the countryside below her. On every side she saw the confused shapes of the other pigeons flying in all directions. Then something white glistened near by. She nearly fell out of the sky with surprise—there was the lighthouse where she had slept, ghostly and familiar in the fog. Now she knew exactly which way to go, and she flew back up the river towards the railway and 35 Station Road as if it was the clearest day she had ever seen.

Mr Potter sat waiting in his kitchen with the rain falling down outside. Again and again he peered through the rain, but the sky was empty, so he hummed a tune to keep himself calm. 'A watched pot never boils', said Mr Potter as he filled the kettle for another cup of tea. Hours passed and the rain went on falling, but the sky was empty. And the rain was still falling, and the sky was still empty as Mr Potter finished his fifth cup of tea.

At last the rain stopped, and a flicker of grey like a speck of ash appeared in the clearing sky. A pigeon. Mr Potter held his breath as it came closer. For a moment it seemed that it was going to fly on overhead, but then it came circling down towards the garden.

Mr Potter ran outside and his pigeon flew gently into his waiting hands. 'My beauty,' he murmured, and then a strange thing happened. Mr Potter heard the sound of beating wings above him. It grew louder and louder, and then all the pigeons that had been lost in the fog came tumbling out from behind the clouds. They had followed Mr Potter's pigeon home. On and on they came, until the lawn was a rustling carpet of grey feathers and the air was filled with soft voices.

So Mr Potter's pigeon came home first, and won the race. Mr Potter laughed behind his moustache and said, 'Who would have thought it?' And who would?

REG CARTWRIGHT, an ex-Art Director, began working with oils thirteen years ago, and is now a full-time painter and illustrator. He has already had three major Exhibitions of his works in a London art gallery. He is particularly fascinated in painting animals and has now completed a second book, *Mrs. Norah's Ark*.

Reg Cartwright's pictures for *Mr. Potter's Pigeon* won the 1980 Mother Goose Award, for ''the most exciting newcomer to British children's book illustration''.

PATRICK KINMONTH, the author, is a journalist for *Vogue* magazine, and is himself becoming increasingly involved in painting.

MR. POTTER'S PIGEON
IS NO ORDINARY PIGEON

What is a *pigeongram*? A message carried by a pigeon! Nowadays we have telephones and telex machines. Aeroplanes, trains, ships and vans carry our letters. Before all these inventions, people often used pigeons to carry messages: not the ordinary pigeons we see living in the woods or city parks, but thoroughbred *homing pigeons.* These remarkable birds are trained to find their way

home from afar, like Mr. Potter's pigeon. Today, they are bred mainly for racing.

Pigeon races take place between April and August. They cover between fifty and one thousand miles. On the eve of a race, the birds are taken to the starting place, and the next morning all are released at the same time. They fly, find their direction, and head fast for home. As the pigeons are at variable distances from their homes, the winner is not the first to get back but the one who reaches the highest average speed.

THE TRAINING

Racing pigeons are carefully reared and trained. The fastest and strongest birds are those chosen for breeding. Before a bird is eight days old, it must be registered with one of the Homing Unions. A ring bearing its registration number, date of birth and place of origin is then fitted to its right leg.

At about six weeks old, the pigeon's training begins. The door of the loft is left open to allow the young birds to explore outside. Usually they do not go far and return when food is brought. The next time they are taken some distance in a basket and released to find their way back.

This happens again and again, and each time from a further distance, until the pigeon is ready for its first race. Sometimes, however, pigeons are lost during training.

HOW DO PIGEONS FIND THEIR WAY?

We do not fully know. The sun appears to be important. On a cloudy day, pigeons tend to get lost, like those in the story, and they do not usally fly at night. The

direction of the wind may also guide them. They have excellent eyesight: their eyes are on the sides of their heads; they can see all around them without turning as we have to do. Pigeons also have a good memory and recognise familiar landmarks, as Mr. Potter's pigeon recognised the lighthouse. But we still do not really understand how a pigeon could find the way from West Africa to Wandsworth!

PIGEON RECORDS

The fastest recorded speed is 110 mph, achieved in a race in 1965. But the winning pigeon was helped by a strong wind. On a windless day 60 mph is probably as fast as a pigeon can fly. The longest recorded homing flight by a pigeon is from a sailing ship off the Ichabo Islands, West Africa, to Wandsworth, London. The pigeon took fifty-five days to fly between 5,400 and 7,000 miles. The poor bird dropped dead a mile from its home.

FLYING POSTMEN

For many centuries homing pigeons acted as flying postmen. They carried messages in capsules fastened to their legs. In Ancient Greece, pigeons carried the names of Olympic Games winners. The people of Paris sent pigeongrams when they were besieged in 1870-1871 during the Franco-Prussian war. In four months pigeons delivered over a million letters to Paris despite the attempts of the Prussians to attack them with hawks. During the Second World War they acted as emergency messengers when radio communication broke down. Today in parts of Britain pigeons are used to deliver blood samples to hospitals. With all the inventions and technology of the twentieth century, it seems that the homing pigeon still can be the fastest and safest carrier!

More Pocket Puffins for you to enjoy!

Bill and Stanley by Helen Oxenbury
*A busy afternoon for Bill and his best friend,
Stanley the dog.*

Peter and the Wolf by Sergei Prokofiev and Erna Voigt
The well-known musical tale, beautifully illustrated.

Panda's Puzzle by Michael Foreman
*Panda travels from the Himalayas to the United States to find
the answer to a very important question.*

Billy Goat and His Well-Fed Friends by N. Hogrogian
Billy Goat doesn't want to end up as the Farmer's supper...

This Little Pig-A-Wig by Lenore and Erik Blegvad
A lovely, lively collection of pig-poems old and new.

The Pearl by Helme Heine
*Beaver realises that there are greater riches in life than even
the loveliest of pearls.*

Fat Pig by Colin McNaughton
*Fat Pig must lose weight. Somehow his friends just have to help
him...*

The Feathered Ogre by Lee Lorenz
*Little Jack the Piper outwits the ferocious ogre and plucks his
golden feathers. A very funny fairy tale.*

If I Had... by Mercer Mayer
*'If only I had a gorilla, a crocodile, a snake...then no-one would
pick on me...' A small boy's daydreams find a real-life solution.*